JULIA JARMAN & ADRIAN REYNOLDS

BIG Bouncy Bed

ORCHARD

Ben and Bella on the big bouncy bed.

Boing!
Boing!
Boing!
Boing!

Mind your head!

Springs go squeak.
Bed goes creak.

But who's that going, "Eek-eek-eek"?

"Hello, kids, is there room for me?"

"Oh yes, Mouse. Come up and see!"

Mouse leaps on and jumps up high.

Covers slip and pillows fly!

Mouse, Ben and Bella on the big bouncy bed.

Boing!

Boing!

Boing!

Boing!

Mind your head!

Springs go squeak.
Bed goes creak.

Mouse is flying —
"Eek-eek-eek!"

Covers slip and pillows fly!

"Who's down there?" Bella cries.

"Hi there, kids! Can I bounce too?"

"Come on up, Kangaroo!"

Kanga leaps. **What a bound!**
Covers slither to the ground!

Mouse, Kanga, Ben and Bella
on the big bouncy bed.

Boing!

Boing! Boing!

BOING! MIND YOUR HEAD!

Feathers flying **everywhere,**

bouncy bed jumps in the air!

But someone's peeping round the door . . .

" . . . Hi there, kids, is there room for more?"

"Course there is, Tiger. Come up and jump."
Tiger springs and the bed goes **bump!**

BUMP, bump, bumpety-bump!

Tiger and Mouse, Kanga, Bella and Ben
on the big bouncy bed,
bouncing high and then . . .

. . . in run Zebra, Dog and Duck.

Kangaroo is panic-struck!
And . . .

...into the room Elephant charges.

"NO!" they cry
as Elephant
barges...

. . . under the bed

hoisting it **high!**

Out through the window . . .

. . . into the **Sky!**

"Wait for me!" Elephant cries.

Then she flaps her ears
and up she flies!
On to the **big bed**, **soaring high**,

Up, up, up

to the starry sky.

Vroom! The bed zooms through the night.
"Everybody hold on tight!
Look at the planets! Look at the stars!

Look at Mercury!

Look at Mars!

Look at Saturn
and the Moon!

There's Jupiter

and there's Neptune!"

"Wow!" cries Bella. "This is ace!
We're whizzing round in outer space!"

"There's planet Venus. Let's land!" yells Ben.

"Too hot!" cries Bella.

"Pluto, then?"

"No, that's too cold,
and there's not enough light.

But that planet there looks just right!"

Planet Earth is all aglow,
like a crystal ball in a magic show!

There's our country!

There's our town!

There's our house!

We're coming . . .

. . . down!
Down!
Down!

Down!

The bed goes **vroom!**

Right back in
to . . .

...Mum and Dad's room!

Dive under the covers.
Pretend to be asleep.

Time to sleep now,
home again.
"Goodnight, Bella.
Goodnight, Ben."